JACK
AND THE
FIRE DRAGON

BY GAIL E. HALEY

Crown Publishers, Inc.
New York

For George and Louise Einhart

and Joy and Don Considine

CROWN is a trademark of Crown Publishers, Inc. Manufactured in Italy.
Library of Congress Cataloging-in-Publication Data
Haley, Gail E. Jack and the Fire Dragon. Summary: Jack encounters the menacing
monster known as Fire Dragaman and rescues three beautiful sisters from the
monster's underground cave. [1. Fairy tales. 2. Folklore—United States] I. Title.
PZ8.H135Jab 1988 398.2'1'0973 [E] 87-24616
ISBN 0-517-56814-4

10 9 8 7 6 5 4 3 2 1

First Edition

Almost any evening there'll be some young'uns at Poppyseed's house. All the wild young things know there's something special about her Story Mountain. You can look out beyond her garden and see the fawns grazin' and pickin'. Possums, skunks, and baby coons will be creepin' up right under her eyes to borrow a little something for dinner.

Not long ago her great-grandchildren, Amy and Todd, came to spend the night. They were helping Poppyseed pick corn when they spotted fiery balls rising up from Brown's Mountain.

"Poppyseed, what are they?"

Poppyseed peered across the valley. "Well, chirrun, no one knows for sure. But some folks say they're Old Fire Dragaman's fireballs. Seems like maybe he's coming back to look for his gals."

Poppyseed started toward the house. "Come help me shuck the corn, and I'll tell you all about it."

Old Fire Dragaman is about the wickedest and biggest giant that ever roamed these hills. Some people believe he dug right up from the center of the earth bringing fire and brimstone with him. Nothin' or nobody could stop him, and no one would live in the places where he hung out. He was famous for takin' people's money and daughters.

Now wouldn't ye know Jack—that reckless feller—would run across him? You all remember Jack, he's that tow-headed scamp lookin' for adventure who always comes young again.

Well, this story happened when Jack's paw and his brothers Tom and Will were back from the war. The family was a-prospering, and Paw bought a tract of new ground for the boys.

Maw packed everything they'd need—quilts, foodstuffs, and cooking utensils. Paw gave them an ox, a sledge, and all the tools they'd need.

"Tom, Will, and Jack," he said, "I want ye to go up and clear enough land for each of ye to have a homestead."

Now Tom and Will had just come back from the war, and they were ready to settle down and start families of their own.

But it was a right long time since Jack had been up the bean tree and met the skyland giants, and he was hankering after some more excitement in his life.

It didn't take the three brothers long to set up a cabin; then it was time to clear the trees off the new ground. It was hard work, so they'd take turns. Each day, one of them would stay at the cabin to do odd jobs and get food ready for the other two.

Tom took the first turn. He was a right good cook from being in the army, and he whipped up a corn pone and some collard greens and fried some big old slices of cured ham.

The smell of that food went drifting down the holler, and it maybe woke somebody up.

Tom was putting up a coatrack behind the door when he heard TROMP, TROMP, TROMP—footsteps coming toward the house. He thought it was just his brothers playing a joke, so he didn't pay it no mind. Well, he should have. Next minute the door flew open and hit him in the head. In come a big old giant on his hands and knees. There wasn't no doubt—it was Fire Dragaman. He gobbled down all the food in one bite, put some coals from the fire into his pipe, and backed out the door. Tom sat down, white as a sheet and clammy as a frog, to wait for his brothers.

Tom was still sittin' by the empty table when Jack and Will come back, hungry as two bears.

"Where in tarnation is our dinner?" they railed at him.

Tom looked at them kind of sickish. "If you'd seen what I seen, you wouldn't want no dinner!" He told them about how Fire Dragaman had eat every bite of the food on the table.

"What? You mean that giant come right up to our cabin and stuck his old head through the door?" Jack and Will shouted. "You're lucky he didn't eat you."

Next day it was Will's turn to stay home and cook. He shot a wild turkey and turned it all day on the spit.

Sure enough, at dinnertime, Old Fire Dragaman turned up again and ate all the food same as he had the day before.

Jack laughed when he heard Will's story, but his brothers said, "You'll laugh out of the other side of your face tomorrow when it's your turn."

Next day, after his brothers had gone, Jack picked some dragon's-blood vines and made a big coil of rope out of them. After that he made a big pot of Hoppin' John and an apple crumble full of cinnamon. He put them at the back of the fireplace to keep warm.

Then he went out on the porch to carve a new axe handle. In the afternoon, he saw a big old tousled head come rarin' up from under the cliffside. Fire Dragaman looked down at Jack with his pipe clenched between his teeth and his greeny eyes round as a cat's.

Jack didn't let on how scared he was; he just looked up right casual-like and said, "Howdy, Daddy."

Seemed like Fire Dragaman had a wind whipping his coat round his knees. He bent way down and looked at Jack. "Howdy, Son."

Jack tried to grin. "Come on in, you're just in time for dinner."

Old Fire Dragaman's eyebrows flew up, and he breathed smoke out of his nose, but he said, "No thankee, I jest come to light my pipe."

"Aw, set for a while and be neighborly," Jack wheedled.

The giant pulled out a jeweled watch as big as a dinner plate. "Got no time," he said. He lit his pipe and was off down the mountain puffin' like three thunderstorms.

Soon as his back was turned, Jack slipped after him. The big feller came to some craggy stones and stepped right down between them. Quick as that, he was gone! Well, Jack wasn't going to let an adventure slip through his hands so easy. He went to the place where the giant had disappeared and looked down into the big, dark cavern. He couldn't see a thing!

Jack went back to the cabin and got there about the same time as his brothers. "What happened, Jack, did ye scare the old giant away?"

"Naw," said Jack, "I asked him to stay for dinner, but he said he was too busy."

Jack told them the story and went off to bed, but the two brothers stayed up late makin' a plot to get even.

Now, the truth is, Jack's brothers were jealous of him. He was the youngest and his mother's pet. And it seemed like he had a way of gettin' out of just about any kind of scrape. So they figured they'd send him down to get some of Fire Dragaman's treasure and not be in no danger themselves.

They took a big old hickory tub and the rope Jack had made out of dragon's-blood vines, and all three of them trooped off to Fire Dragaman's hole. They tied the rope onto the tub.

"Jack, you're the lightest," said Tom and Will. "Get in the bucket, and we'll lower you down. When you want to come up, jerk on the rope, and we'll pull you up."

Jack got in the bucket, and they lowered him down, down, down. He couldn't see a thing. When the bucket finally touched bottom, Jack got out. It was almost as light as day. Some kind of light was coming out of the rocks themselves.

Jack took a few steps away from the tub, and there below he saw Fire Dragaman's house, looking like it had grown right out of the rocks. "Bedad," said Jack, "I never saw no house as big as that!"

He had to cross an underground river to get there. On the porch, he found a pretty girl spinning at a wheel. Jack was too tongue-tied to talk to her, but he remembered a song his mother sang.

Pretty girl with shining hair,
Tell me, what's your name?
I'll save you from this dragon's den
And take you home again.

"My name's Annabelle. I'll gladly go with you, but you must save my two sisters as well."

Jack agreed and took her out to the tub. He pulled the rope two times, and up she went. "Go into the house," she called out. "There you'll find my sister Marie."

Jack went into the house and found a girl who was twice as pretty as Annabelle mending Fire Dragaman's big socks.

Marie said, "I'd be glad to get out of this place, but you must come back for our little sister Jenny. She's out in the kitchen peeling taters."

Jack sent Marie up in the bucket and went back for Jenny.

Jack found Jenny in the kitchen. She was so beautiful that she lit up the whole room, and Jack fell in love with her on the spot. Jenny was right taken with Jack, too. The truth is, she'd never seen a young man before. She told Jack how Fire Dragaman had stolen her when she was just a baby and her sisters were little bitty young'uns.

"I'd sure like to marry you, Jenny," said Jack as bold as brass.

"I'd like that too, Jack," she said, and she let him plait a red ribbon in her hair to show that she was engaged. She took a sparkling ring from a chain about her neck and placed it on his finger. "They say there's magic in this ring, Jack. It has the power to grant wishes to the brave and true of heart."

Jenny went to a large trunk near the fireplace, opened it, and took out a little bottle of sweet-smelling salve. "The cream in this bottle is magic. If Fire Dragaman comes back, he'll throw fireballs at ye. This is the only thing that will keep you from burning up."

Jenny reached down into the trunk again and pulled out a silver sword. "This sword is called Dragonteaser. It's the only thing in the world that can hurt Fire Dragaman."

Jack took Jenny out to the tub. He gave her a kiss and tugged on the rope twice. Soon she was rising up, up, and out of sight.

On the ground above, Tom and Will were courtin' Annabelle and Marie. But when they saw Jenny, they forgot about her sisters and commenced to fight over her.

Jenny wrung her hands. "Stop that, you two; I can't stand fightin'. And besides, I've already promised to marry Jack."

"Well, blame it all, he can just stay down there!" said Will angrily, and he chucked the rope back down the hole.

Jack saw what a fix he was in. The rock was too steep for him to climb, and he was trapped. He headed back to the giant's house looking for another way out.

It wasn't long before Fire Dragaman come snortin' and puffin' from some cave down below. He saw Jack right away, crouching down with Dragonteaser in his hand.

"Howdy, neighbor," he snarled. "I reckon ye come for to steal my girls, and maybe some of my gold. Take 'em if ye're man enough." That old giant was fearsome enough when he was up on the earth in broad daylight. But down in his cave under the earth, he had the power to change himself into a slinky, scaly fire-breathing dragon. And that's just what he did—right before Jack's eyes.

It was enough to scare anyone—even a reckless feller like Jack!

Fire Dragon raised up his scaly head and spit a fireball at Jack the size of a honeydew. Jack smacked it broadside with his sword. The sparks come down all over Jack and burned holes in his shirt and skin. It plumb knocked him off his feet.

It was all Jack could do to get out the magic ointment and smear it on the burned places. Soon as he did, the pain went away, the burns disappeared, and Jack felt twice as strong as before.

The next fireball was so big it went clean through the wall of the house. As fast as the flames came, Jack kept smearing the ointment on his burns.

Now it was Fire Dragon's turn to be skeered. He could see that the fire of battle was in Jack. It was shining from his eyes and gleaming off the blade of Dragonteaser.

He stoked up his furnace as high as it would go and flung even worse fireballs at Jack. He slashed at him with his sharp claws and his spiky tail.

Fire Dragon's power started to give out—his fireballs were getting smaller, but Jack seemed as strong as ever.

Jack moved in on him closer and closer. "If ye kill me, I'll come back to haint ye, Jack," puffed the dragon.

Jack raised Dragonteaser and plunged it right through the giant's heart.

Phzzzzzz. The dragon fizzled away till nothing was left but a giant fireball that drifted down the cave in the direction of the river.

"I'll be baackk, Jaackkk . . ." the old giant's voice echoed along the walls of the cave.

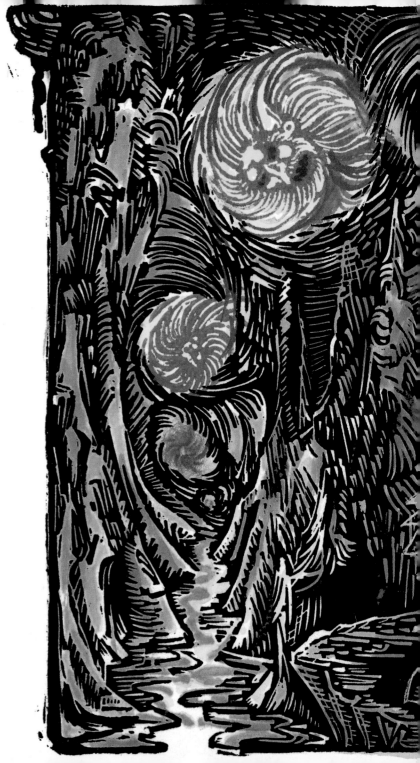

Jack's clothes were burned to tatters. He was feeling pretty hungry, but he couldn't find much food—only some stale bread and the taters Jenny had been peeling.

He remembered what Fire Dragaman had said about gold, and as he searched for a way out, he found enough treasure to make ten men rich. He filled a sack with gold and pretty trinkets for Jenny.

After three days, he still hadn't found a way out. He sat down and held onto the sword Jenny had given him. He thought about her blue eyes.

"Reckon I'm gonna starve and die down here, Jenny," he whispered. "I sure do wish I was up there with you."

Now Jack had clean forgot about the wishing ring.

Whooosh—in an instant, he was back at the cabin.

His brothers were still fighting over Jenny, but when they saw Jack, stronger and handsomer than before, swinging Dragonteaser over his head, they stopped where they stood and goggled at him with their mouths open like two old bullfrogs.

When Jack saw how funny they looked, he started laughing. He liked laughing better than he liked fighting. So he forgave his rotten brothers. It wasn't the first trick they'd played on him, and he reckoned it wouldn't be the last.

Jenny come running and hugged his neck. She was still wearing the red ribbon in her hair. He took one look at her and knew he had the prettiest gal in the world for his wife. With his pockets full of the giant's treasure and Dragon-teaser to hang on his wall, he was ready to settle down for a while, because for once he'd had enough excitement. Tom married Annabelle, Will married Marie, and they was all gettin' on fine the last time I saw them.

On certain special nights, the fireballs still rise over Brown's Mountain. People have many stories about what they are and where they come from, but Poppyseed has no doubts.

Stop by her house, next time you're up this way. She never runs out of stories about Jack, that tow-headed scamp who keeps turning young again.